Where Does God Live?

Holly Bea

Illustrated by Kim Howard

H J Kramer
Starseed Press
Tiburon, California

For Heather, Katie, Megan, Natalie,
and all God's children.
H.B.

For my sweet baby,
Amelia Ruby Howard.
K.H.

Library of Congress Cataloging-in-Publication Data

Bea, Holly, 1956–
  Where does God live? / Holly Bea; illustrated by Kim Howard
    p.   cm.
  Summary: A young girl learns from her grandmother that she can
find God all around her.
  ISBN 0–915811–73–1
  [1. God—Fiction.   2. Stories in rhyme.]   I. Howard, Kim, ill.
II. Title.   96–30382
PZ8.3.B3485Wh   1997   CIP
[E]—dc20   AC

H J Kramer Inc
Starseed Press
P.O. Box 1082
Tiburon, CA 94920
Printed in Singapore.
10 9 8 7 6 5 4

This is Hope. She's a lot like you.
She loves her puppy and the color blue.
She likes to laugh and play and sing,
But asking questions is her favorite thing.

"Where does the sun go? Why does it rain?
Why don't snowflakes all look the same?"
There were so many things Hope wanted to know,
Such as "How many colors are in a rainbow?"

She'd ask her friends, and her mom and dad,
Her Grandmother Rose, and her big brother Brad.
The mailman, the grocer, and nice Mrs. Ying—
She'd ask anyone about any old thing.

One day a new question popped into her head,
And she asked her mom (who was making the bed),
"Where does God live? Does God live nearby?"
"Hope, God lives in Heaven, way up in the sky."

Now Hope hadn't heard about Heaven before,
But she knew that she wanted to learn a lot more.
So she went to the meadow to have a few words
With sweet Mrs. Peep, her favorite bird.
"Have you ever seen Heaven, way up in the sky?
Have you ever seen God when you fly far and high?"

"I've seen clouds and stars and skies of blue,
The moon and rainbows and lightning, too.
I've never seen Heaven though I've flown far and near,
But the sky is so lovely, God has to live here."

Hope thanked Mrs. Peep and went down to the stream
To see Mr. Frog, who was chubby and green.
"Where does God live?" she asked Mr. Frog.
He looked up and smiled as he sat on his log.

"Look at the flowers, the wide open spaces,
The trees and the butterflies—these beautiful places!
To me, this is almost like Heaven, you see.
That's how I know that God lives here with me."

All of a sudden and quick as a flash,
Mrs. Fish jumped up high and came down with a splash.
"Oh no, that's not true! That can't really be!
I know that God lives in the stream here with me.
This crystal blue water is lovely, I know.
God lives here with me in the waters below."

Hope thanked her friends and went on her way
To hear what her grandmother might have to say.
Her grandma was wise and her heart very pure,
And she'd know the answer, of that Hope was sure.

"Does God live in Heaven, or down by the stream?
Does God live in the water, or is God a dream?
Tell me where does God live—I really must know.
Oh please, won't you tell me, my sweet Grandma Rose?"

Her grandmother smiled, as grandmothers can,
And softly she reached out for Hope's little hand.
"I know you're confused, and I'm glad that you came.
Now listen real close, and I'll try to explain.

"You know God made everything, seen and unseen,
The wind and the sun and the meadow so green.
Flowers and stars and oceans of blue.
Trees, birds, and rocks, and all people, too.

"And when God makes a person, a star, or a wave,
A part of God stays with whatever God's made.
So God lives in the sky, in the meadow and stream—
God lives everywhere, and God isn't a dream.

"God lives in the frogs and the birds and in you.
When you're looking for God, it's easy to do.
God lives in all things that you see, hear, or touch.
God lives in all people. God's in each one of us.

"And when you meet people who are loving and good,
They're letting God out, just as everyone could.
And if you meet people who seem hateful or bad,
They've forgotten God's here, and that makes God sad.

"God is gentle and loving and cares for us all.
God gives us the strength to get up when we fall.
God is always around to help us find truth,
Whether we're old or still in our youth.

"God's your best friend, Hope—God really cares—
So make sure every day to take time for your prayers."
"How should I pray, Grandma? What should I say?
I want God to hear me. What's the best way?"

Her grandmother hugged her and said, "Precious you!
Just speak from your heart, Hope. It's easy to do.
Tell God your wishes, your fears, and your dreams,
Then thank God for all of your favorite things.
Ask God to guide you in all that you do,
And be thankful for all of the love God sends you."

Hope kissed Grandma Rose and went on her way.
She had no more questions—at least for that day.
And on her way home, she saw God in all things,
In the clouds and the flowers—and in nice Mrs. Ying.

And later that night when Hope went to bed,
She closed her eyes slowly and bowed down her head.
"Dear God, thank you so much for this wonderful day.
Thanks for the friends who showed me the way.
Please help me tomorrow in all that I do,
And don't forget, God, how much I love you."